Dear Reader,

This book was made completely by me, Jake Cake. I did all the words and all the pictures and it took me ages. It's about all the strange things that get me into trouble. Strange things that are SO STRANGE no one EVER believes me.

When I try telling grown-ups what REALLY happened they shake their heads and say: 'DON'T MAKE UP STORIES OR YOUR NOSE WILL GROW LONG!'

But I'm not making up stories. Everything I'm about to tell you is true. It all REALLY HAPPENED!

signed Jake Cake

Michael Broad spent much of his childhood gazing out of the window imagining he was somewhere more interesting.

Now he's a grown-up Michael still spends a lot of time gazing out of the window imagining he's somewhere more interesting – but now he writes and illustrates books as well.

Some of them are picture books, like *Broken Bird* and *The Little Star Who Wished*.

michaelbroad.co.uk

Books by Michael Broad

JAKE CAKE: THE FOOTBALL BEAST
JAKE CAKE: THE PIRATE CURSE
JAKE CAKE: THE ROBOT DINNER LADY
JAKE CAKE: THE SCHOOL DRAGON
JAKE CAKE: THE VISITING VAMPIRE
JAKE CAKE: THE WEREWOLF TEACHER

JAKE CAKE

THE ROBOT DINNER LADY

Michael Broad

PUFFIN

PUFFIN BOOKS

Published by the Penguin Group
Penguin Books Ltd, 80 Strand, London WC2R 0RL, England
Penguin Group (USA) Inc., 375 Hudson Street, New York, New York 10014, USA
Penguin Group (Canada), 90 Eglinton Avenue East, Suite 700, Toronto, Ontario, Canada M4P 2Y3
(a division of Pearson Penguin Canada Inc.)
Penguin Ireland, 25 St Stephen's Green, Dublin 2, Ireland (a division of Penguin Books Ltd)
Penguin Group (Australia), 250 Camberwell Road, Camberwell, Victoria 3124, Australia
(a division of Pearson Australia Group Pty Ltd)
Penguin Books India Pvt Ltd, 11 Community Centre, Panchsheel Park, New Delhi – 110 017, India
Penguin Group (NZ), 67 Apollo Drive, Mairangi Bay, Auckland 1310, New Zealand
(a division of Pearson New Zealand Ltd)
Penguin Books (South Africa) (Pty) Ltd, 24 Sturdee Avenue, Rosebank, Johannesburg 2196, South Africa

Penguin Books Ltd, Registered Offices: 80 Strand, London WC2R 0RL, England

penguin.com

Published 2007
8

Set in Perpetua by Palimpsest Book Production Limited,
Polmont, Stirlingshire
Made and printed in England by Clays Ltd, St Ives plc

British Library Cataloguing in Publication Data
A CIP catalogue record for this book is available from the British Library

ISBN: 978-0-141-32088-5

www.greenpenguin.co.uk

Penguin Books is committed to a sustainable future
for our business, our readers and our planet.
The book in your hands is made from paper
certified by the Forest Stewardship Council.

Here are three UNBELIEVABLE stories about the times I met:

JAKE CAKE
AND THE
ROBOT DINNER LADY

In class before dinner time one of two smells will waft under the door: either the delicious smell of chips or the rotten stink of cabbage.

me Smelling

CHIPS

If it's chips you know it'll either be burger and chips, fish fingers and chips or pizza and chips. But if it's cabbage you know it'll either be mince and cabbage, liver and cabbage or even cabbage and cabbage (if you don't join the queue early!).

me Smelling

Cabbage

Today it was cabbage, which didn't come as a huge surprise because it had been cabbage for the past two weeks and I was beginning to forget what chips smelled like!

Mrs Brown the new dinner lady was to blame. She'd taken over the school kitchen exactly two weeks ago and not a single chip had been seen since then. As the dinner bell rang and a dozen chairs scraped the floor, the thought of yet another plate of steaming, green mush made me groan loudly and flop forward on my desk in protest.

'JAKE CAKE!' yelled Mrs Winter. 'Have your batteries run down?'

'No, Mrs Winter,' I said, lifting my head a fraction. Mrs Winter is our science teacher, so she'd probably know if my batteries had run down, and if they had, she'd probably clip wires to my ears and charge me up again.

'Good! Then you won't mind taking this note to Mrs Brown immediately!' she said, scribbling frantically in her notepad and waving the square of paper in the air.

As I dragged myself up to the front of the classroom and took the note I noticed a mischievous look on Mrs Winter's face, and when I got outside and read the note I found out why!

mischievous
Look
K

This is what it said:

Dear Mrs Brown,
   Could you please give Jake Cake a double helping of cabbage and make sure he eats every last morsel. The poor boy's energy levels were dreadfully low in class today and therefore he's clearly in need of more delicious green vegetables!
   Yours sincerely
   Mrs Winter
   P.S. Jake, it is very rude to read other people's notes!

I should have known better than to mess with Mrs Winter. She's the one who made me stay behind after school for making up stories about headless horsemen playing polo on the football field (I didn't make it up, it really happened! But I'll tell you about that another time).

In the canteen all the kids looked miserable as they carried cabbage-heavy plates to their tables, and towering above everyone was Mrs Brown,

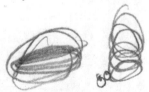

merrily slopping out the soggy green
leaves from a large vat at her side.

She was very tall and very wide, like
a tank in a dress.

I sighed heavily and passed the piece
of paper to Mrs
Brown.

'MORE CABBAGE!' she boomed
excitedly, and ladled a giant helping
of stinky green leaves on my plate.
'MORE CABBAGE GOOD!'
I mumbled a reluctant, 'Thank
you,' and was about to move away
when Mrs Brown
gripped my arm in
a vice-like grip.

VICE-LIKE GRIP!

'*MORE* CABBAGE!' she boomed
again, and continued to fill my plate.

Mrs Brown went on filling my plate
until eventually the cabbage mountain
grew so large it started spilling over the
side, and *still* she piled it on. Stiff green
leaves with thick white veins, soggy
yellow leaves that were limp and mushy,
great chunks of the-white-bit-in-the-
middle that makes a horrible
crunching sound in your mouth.
Every disgusting part of the

cabbage tumbled on to my plate, over the edge and on to the floor in a great green fountain of foulness.

The plate was so heavy it swayed backwards and forwards and, as I tried to steady my hand, I noticed Mrs Brown turn her head to follow it. With one hand clamped to my arm and the other working double time with the ladle, her sights were fixed only on the plate and wherever it moved she followed.

As her grip on my arm grew tighter and the ladle sped up I knew the only way to escape the cycle of cabbage would be to put my 'plate theory' to the test. I would of course get into tons of trouble, but what else could I do?

The grim determination on Mrs
Brown's face left me no choice.

So I took a deep breath and lobbed
the plate over the back of my head.

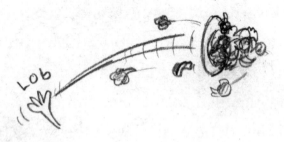

I watched carefully as Mrs Brown's
eyes widened to track the arc of its
flight path. Suddenly she dropped my
arm and leapt right over my head after it.

That dinner lady must have jumped
nearly two metres in the air!

15

I expected to hear the clattering of
my plate hitting the floor, or the splat
of falling cabbage, maybe even the thud
of a falling dinner lady. But instead I
heard a voice, a very loud and very
angry voice that silenced the
whole canteen.

'JAKE CAKE! WHAT ON EARTH DO YOU THINK YOU'RE DOING?'

Turning around, I saw all the other kids frozen to the spot with their mouths hanging open. But they weren't looking at the dinner lady, they were looking at Mrs Winter who stood in the middle of the canteen with my plate on her head!

GULP!

Shaking with
fury Mrs Winter
slowly took the plate
from her head, swept the
food from her face and spoke in
a calm, level tone that was
somehow even scarier than shouting.

'Jake Cake, will you please go and
wait for me in my classroom,' she said.

Leaving the canteen with my head
hung low, I glanced back at Mrs
Brown. She was gazing at her ladle and
looking confused. No one was paying
her any attention, which meant *everyone*
had been watching the flying plate and
no one had been watching the flying
dinner lady!

No one would EVER believe what she'd done.

As I sat on my own in Mrs Winter's classroom I tried to piece it all together.

THUD
THUD
THU D

There was definitely something going on with Mrs Brown. No dinner lady could be THAT into cabbage, and more importantly no dinner lady, not even a really big one, should be able to jump over your head!

Soon I heard loud angry footsteps making their way down the hall and my heart sank. I guessed Mrs Winter must be *really* cross to make so much racket. But as the footsteps drew closer and heavier, and the desks and chairs began shaking and quaking, it occurred to me that it might not be Mrs Winter at all . . . The door exploded inwards and Mrs Brown filled the doorway, a ladle in one hand, a plate in

the other and the large vat of cabbage
strapped to her back!

'JAKE CAKE, MORE CABBAGE!'
she boomed, and stormed into the
classroom, bringing most of the
door frame with her.

'ARRRRRRGH!' I yelled and leapt from my desk, but there was nowhere for me to run to. I was trapped in the classroom with a crazed and freakishly strong dinner lady!

Mrs Brown scooped a great heap of cabbage from over her shoulder, slopped it on to the plate and charged towards me.

'MORE! MORE! MORE!' came her thundering war cry.

I stumbled to the back of the class with the dinner lady almost on top of me.

I hit the wall and pressed my back flat against it. There was nowhere left to go. She had me cornered.

'MORE CABBAGE FOR JAKE CAKE!' Mrs Brown grinned, and with

the plate held high she took one final
step towards me. But her grin became
a confused frown as her shoe slid on a
slimy green leaf and suddenly
the giant dinner lady
was back up in
the air again!

Mrs Brown somersaulted through a
shower of green leaves and landed on
her bottom! But she
didn't land on her bottom
with a soft thud. She didn't even land
on her bottom with a loud thud. The
noise Mrs Brown made as she landed

CLANG!

on her bottom could only be described
as an almighty CLANG!

I held my breath for a moment
because I didn't know what to do.
Even though Mrs Brown was big and
scary and broke down
doors, I was still
worried about her. Normally
when someone falls over you check to
see if they've broken something,

· but with the noise Mrs
Brown made it seemed more likely
she had *dented* something!

'Are you OK, Mrs Brown?'
I asked, carefully moving closer.

'Bzzzzz!' replied Mrs Brown.

'Have you dented anything?' I asked,
crouching down beside her.

'Wrrrrrr!' replied Mrs Brown.

'Shall I fetch the school nurse?'
I asked, leaning in closer.

Suddenly Mrs Brown made a loud
bang, sparks shot out of her ears and
her head rolled off her shoulders on to
the floor with another big CLANG!

'ARRRRRGGGGHHH!' I screamed,
and legged it for the door.

But I only got halfway before I
realized that heads – and bottoms for
that matter – don't make CLANGING!
sounds (which is a scientific fact, and

Mrs Winter would have been pleased with my observation if she wasn't already angry about the plate of cabbage on her head).

Feeling almost certain that the only things that made CLANGING! sounds were things made of metal, I went back to Mrs Brown.

I picked up the head and studied it. I turned it around in my hands and studied it some more, then I tapped the top of it with the ladle and the dinner lady's head went CLANG! CLANG! CLANG! like a rusty old saucepan.

Mrs Brown was a robot! A real-life, oil-drinking, non-human ROBOT!

I had one of two choices. I could either leave the robot dinner lady where she was, without a head, and no doubt get the blame for breaking her and probably get into loads more trouble. Or I could try to fix her and then leg it. Then Mrs Winter would see Mrs Brown on the rampage and would definitely realize that none of it was my fault.

I found a couple of wires dangling out of Mrs Brown's head so I plugged them back in and screwed the whole thing back on to her shoulders. Her mouth and eyelids made a funny

clicking sound and flicked open, but she still wasn't moving or saying anything.

I tried tapping her on the head with the ladle again. My mum bangs the TV when it plays up and it usually works, but nothing happened to the robot.

As I tap-tap-tapped away on Mrs Brown's head I suddenly became aware of someone standing in the doorway (or what was left of the doorway). And there was Mrs Winter, with a mixture of confusion and horror on her face, as she watched me clanging away on the big heap of dinner lady!

'It wasn't my fault!' I blurted out. 'She's a robot and she jumped over my head and then broke the door and

slipped up on the cabbage and then her head fell off and I stuck it back on and . . .!'

Mrs Winter waved my excuses away with a flick of her hand, pulled out a set of spanners from her desk drawer and strode towards me and the broken dinner lady.

'If anyone was likely to get into trouble with Mrs Brown I had a funny feeling it might be you, Jake Cake,' she said, as she unbolted a panel on the robot's back.

'You *knew* she was a robot!' I said.

'Of course I knew,' Mrs Winter chuckled, as she surveyed the mess of robot workings spilling from the dinner lady's back. 'I *have* spent the last five years making her.'

'Oh,' I said, because I couldn't think of anything else to say.

'Oh, indeed!' said Mrs Winter, pulling at a bunch of loose wires and studying each connection in turn. 'But it would seem one extra helping of cabbage was all it took to overload her system.'

'So it wasn't really my fault?' I said.

'Well, you did make her jump over your head, which she wasn't really designed to do,' said Mrs Winter with a frown. 'But no, I suppose it wasn't your fault. Something must have got into her system.'

I watched as Mrs Winter pulled out a small circuit board with dozens of coloured wires attached to tiny coloured circuits and little grey microchips. She traced her finger over the surface until she found what she was looking for.

'AHA!' said Mrs Winter, pulling out a tiny sliver of green with the tips of her fingers. She studied it closely and sighed. 'It would seem all my hard work has been sabotaged by a tiny piece of cabbage.'

'But you can make her work again?' I asked, because when I thought about it I decided having a robot dinner lady was actually pretty cool.

'I suppose I could,' said Mrs Winter,

as we dragged the dinner lady into the
stationery cupboard. 'But it would be
only a matter of time before another
bit of cabbage slithered its way into
her system. Robots are very sensitive,
you know.'

As Mrs Winter locked the door I
suddenly had an idea.

'Couldn't you programme Mrs Brown to cook something else, something not so slimy?' I asked, and tried not to sound too excited. Grown-ups get suspicious when kids get excited about something so you have to pretend that you don't really care. 'Chips wouldn't get into her circuits,' I suggested innocently. 'But I don't suppose Mrs Brown is *clever enough* to cook chips . . .'

'Clever enough?' shrieked Mrs Winter, sounding very offended.

'Well, chips are much harder to cook than cabbage,' I said. 'They might be too difficult. Mrs Brown is just a robot . . .'

'Just a robot! I could programme Mrs Brown to make *perfect* chips if I wanted to!' Mrs Winter strode over to the blackboard and started mapping out diagrams and calculations to prove her theory. As the chalk scratched and scribbled up and down the board I smiled to myself. It seemed Mrs Winter *could* be messed with after all!

The following day Mrs Winter had dark rings round her eyes as though she hadn't had much sleep (in fact she looked as though *her* batteries had run down), and when the delicious smell of chips wafted under the classroom door I knew why.

Mrs Winter had spent all night programming Mrs Brown to make perfect chips! She also programmed her *not* to make cabbage any more just to be on the safe side. And because nothing else got into her circuit board Mrs Brown never went on the rampage again, which is a shame because now no one ever believes me when I tell them my dinner lady is a robot.

They just say: 'JAKE CAKE, DON'T MAKE UP STORIES OR YOUR NOSE WILL GROW LONG!' But I wouldn't mind a long nose, especially if the smell of chips wafts under the door.

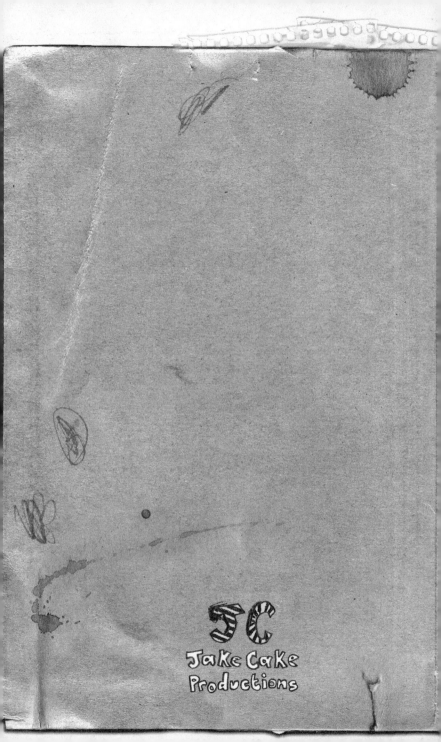

JC

Jake Cake
Productions

JAKE CAKE

AND THE

GARDEN GOBLINS

6'6"		6'6"
6'0"		6'0"
5'6"		5'6"
5'0"		5'0"
4'6"		4'6"
4'0"		4'0"
3'6"		3'6"
3'0"		3'0"

There's a shed at the bottom of our garden I call the JCHQ, which stands for the Jake Cake Headquarters.

JC HQ ↑

It's my own private den where I write all the stories, draw all the pictures and file away evidence from my adventures.

The JCHQ is my favourite place in the whole wide world. The best thing about it is NO GROWN-UPS ARE ALLOWED INSIDE, and Mum and

Dad go along with this rule
because they say it keeps me out
of mischief.

I spend all my spare time in the
JCHQ; all my spare time except for
Saturday mornings. I always watch TV
on Saturday mornings
because there's loads of
good stuff on for kids.

It was a Saturday morning when Mum
came into the living room and stood
in front of the TV, waving a bucket
and a pair of gardening gloves.

'Wouldn't you rather be out in the
sunshine, Angel Cake?' Mum said
cheerily.

'No, thanks,' I said, leaning sideways
and craning my neck to see the screen.
  'Not even to do a bit of weeding for
your mum?' she added hopefully,
moving to block my view again.

'No, thanks,' I said,
craning in the
opposite direction.
Although by now I
could already feel my
Saturday-morning TV
slipping from my grip.

'Not even if I *pay* you?' Mum added with slumped shoulders and a heavy sigh.

I looked up from the TV and raised an interested eyebrow.

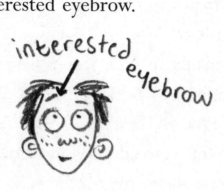

interested eyebrow

As I said before I spend most of my time in the JCHQ and sometimes I need to earn extra cash to buy paper, pens and anything else I need to make my books. That's when I do chores for Mum, even if it means sacrificing my Saturday-morning routine.

Weeding is not the kind of thing you would think could get you into trouble (though I once did battle with a man-eating rose bush and got into loads of trouble for chopping it down, but I'll tell you about that another time). So after a bit of

Man-eating rose bush

negotiation I agreed to take the job.

Mum handed over the gardening gloves and bucket and off I went. But as soon as I stepped into the garden to make a start I heard strange noises coming from the shed.

RUSTLE RUSTLE

Someone or something was rustling around inside the JCHQ!

Mum and Dad were clearing out the garage so I knew it couldn't be them breaking the 'no grown-ups' rule. I crept up to the shed, cupped my gloved hands around the small dusty window and peered inside to investigate.

With my nose squidged against
the glass I saw the reason for
the rustling. All my papers and folders
and notebooks were flying around the
shed as if a mini
tornado was going
off inside! At
first I thought
the JCHQ might
be haunted.

Throwing stuff around is
usually the sort of thing
mischievous ghosts get up
to, but ghosts don't
normally come out
during the day so it had
to be something else.

Watching closely I suddenly caught a glimpse of something: a small dark shadow swinging from shelf to shelf, pulling out files, opening them up and flinging all the pages into the air. Then I saw another one, and another one. It was impossible to see exactly what they were but I knew I had to get inside before they ruined all my work.

I moved round to the shed door and flung it open to catch the mysterious creatures in the act.

It kind of worked
because the shed fell silent
except for a few loose pages
fluttering to the ground. But there
was no sign of whatever had caused
the damage.

'Hello?' I said, stepping cautiously
inside and peering into the gloom.

Suddenly a small gruff voice
yelled, 'LEG IT, MEN!' and a dozen
tiny figures sprang from a dozen tiny
hiding places and shot through my
legs towards the door.

55

Luckily I was still holding the latch and quick as a flash I pulled the door shut so they couldn't escape. A dozen tiny yelps followed a dozen tiny thuds as they crashed straight into the door and landed on top of each other, and when I looked down I saw a dozen tiny green men cursing and shaking their tiny green fists at me!

GOBLINS!!!

The goblins were about the height of a half-chewed pencil. They all had rough green skin and scruffy grey hair with scruffy grey beards to match. All except one who just had a scruffy moustache, which was all curled up at the edges and nearly as big as his head. I stared down at them with my mouth open until I suddenly realized they were all staring back at me, looking very angry.

The one with the moustache was tapping
his foot impatiently on the floor.

I don't know what you're
supposed to do or say when
you find goblins ransacking
your shed, so I just said the first thing
that came into my head.

'You're goblins!' I gasped.

The goblins said nothing.

'*Real* goblins!' I added, crouching
down to get a closer look.

I'd never seen
anything quite
like them
before so I
reached out to
poke one to
make sure they were real.

DON'T EVER DO THIS TO A
GOBLIN!

He immediately snapped at my hand
with his sharp little teeth and bit a
hole in the tough
gardening gloves.

'Hey!' I said,
'There's no need
to bite, I won't
hurt you.'

'Then let us go!' demanded the goblin
with the curly moustache who looked
as though he might be their leader.

'Not before you tell me what you
were all doing in my shed,' I said,
looking at all the papers thrown across

the desk and the
floor, and wondering
how long it would
take to file them all
away again.

A ripple of shrugs swept through the mob of little men, then they all turned to the goblin with the big moustache (definitely the leader). He was now shuffling uncomfortably from one foot to the other.

'Well?' I added impatiently.

'Um,' said the goblin leader, staring at the floor and suddenly looking very sheepish. 'We were bored.'

'BORED!' I yelled, and then felt bad for raising my voice because it made the goblins jump back.

I quickly changed my tone and said, 'Bored?' more calmly and with a question mark on the end.

The goblin leader stepped forward and put his arms into the air the way toddlers do when they want to be picked up. I picked him up and brought the little man to my eye level.

'It's not our fault,' said the goblin, pacing up and down my hand. 'It's just that goblins have lots of energy on account of being so small and sometimes we get a bit overenthusiastic.'

'But what were you doing in my shed in the first place?' I asked.

'We were going from shed to shed looking for an old television. Big folk usually put old things in their sheds and then forget about them. It's where we get most of our stuff – very low-risk looting,' he explained. 'Yours was the last shed in the street and we got a bit fed up.'

'Why were you looking for a television?' I asked.

'Watching TV is our favourite thing!' said the leader. 'But we can only usually do it at night when the big folk are in bed. It's much too risky in the daytime. So we decided to find one of our own.'

'You watch *our* televisions when we're in bed?' I gasped.

'We get in through the letter box and watch late-night horror films!' He grinned, and the other goblins started jumping up and down excitedly.

'TV! TV! TV!' they chanted.

These guys *really* liked watching TV.

I thought about all the Saturday-morning TV *I* was missing and about the gardening I was supposed to be doing. Then I looked at the goblins-with-too-much-energy and had a brilliant idea.

'I'll make a deal with you,' I said.

The deal was that the goblins could come inside the house and watch TV with me until all the Saturday-morning kids' programmes were over. In return they would help with the gardening and get it all done before Mum and Dad finished the garage.

The goblins huddled together, whispering. Eventually the leader nodded and held out his hand to me. I crouched down, shook his hand to seal the deal and then led the little green men into the house.

You might think that's where the trouble started.

I agree that letting a bunch of hyperactive goblins into your house doesn't sound like the cleverest idea in the world, especially with Mum and Dad only two rooms away in the garage. OK, they did get very excited watching the cartoons, but apart from swinging from the lampshade, and using the sofa as a trampoline (and one goblin who had a wee in one of

Mum's plant pots),
they were generally
very well behaved.
You might now be
thinking that the
trouble started when
the TV programmes
were over, when the
goblins had to do some work. I did
wonder whether they would scarper,
never to be seen again. But when we
got outside the goblins leapt around
enthusiastically, waiting for me to tell
them what to do.

Goblins really
do have too much
energy!

'We have to weed the garden,' I said, setting down the empty bucket.

The goblins looked at the bucket and scratched their heads. They all seemed genuinely confused.

'What's "weeding the garden"?' asked the leader.

I pointed at the flower beds. 'It just means pulling out all the bad plants so all the good plants can grow properly,' I said, feeling pleased with myself that I'd summed it up so simply.

'We can take care of that, no problem at all.' The goblin whistled through his fingers and all the other goblins formed an orderly line before him. 'You heard him, lads. Let's get cracking!'

The other goblins nodded obediently and shot away into the flower beds, dragging the bucket behind them.

'We'll have it done in no time,' the leader stated confidently and headed out after them to supervise.

With nothing else to do I decided to tackle the mess in the shed, and because I could hear the goblins huffing and puffing, and the leader calling out various instructions to his workers,

made a mistake

I was happy to leave them to it.

And *that* was where the trouble started!

I'd just finished sorting out the mess in the shed when I heard someone tapping on the door. I opened it to find the goblins waiting outside, looking very pleased with themselves. But when the leader showed me the weeding bucket I nearly screamed out loud.

It was full of mangled flowers!

With a sinking feeling in my stomach
I stepped from the shed and looked
around the garden in horror. Every
single flower was gone from Mum's
borders, and all the shrubs and bushes
had been uprooted and
plonked on the
compost heap!

Compost Heap

'What have you done?' I gasped.

'We have weeded out all the useless plants from your garden,' the leader stated proudly. The other goblins smiled at me and nodded.

'But these aren't the weeds!' I pleaded, waving the bucket in the air. 'You've pulled out all the wrong ones!' Then I noticed that not only were all the weeds still in the flower beds, but they had also been pruned and watered and spaced out in neat little rows.

empty garden

'Oh.' The goblin leader scratched his head and frowned. 'But you told us to take out all the useless plants, and flowers are the most useless plants of all.'

'Uh?' I said, because I was still kind of in shock.

'Well, you can't eat flowers, or make clothes out of them, and worst of all they smell really horrible. So we left you all the yummy dandelions, bouncy moss, nettles for playing *Sting Ball* and all the other wild plants that . . .' the leader's eyes grew wide as realization suddenly dawned '. . . that I suppose big folk would consider *weeds*.'

The goblins looked very sorry, but not as sorry as I was that *all* Mum's plants and flowers had been ripped out and piled on to the stinky compost heap! And as bad luck would have it, that's when Mum appeared with a plate of sandwiches and a glass of lemonade.

Mum looked around the garden. Her jaw dropped, and so did the lemonade and sandwiches — on to the grass at her feet.

She seemed stunned for a moment and glancing around I noticed all the goblins had legged it. I'd like to have legged it too but knew I had to stay and face the wrath of Mum.

'WHAT HAVE YOU DONE TO MY BEAUTIFUL FLOWERS?' Mum shrieked, staggering over to the compost heap. She picked up a single wilted rose bush and gazed sadly at it. 'But it wasn't me, it was . . .'

I stopped and realized how it
would sound if I told the truth,
and even if I did tell the truth it
was still my fault because I should
have done the weeding myself. So I
just stood there with my mouth open.

 'Well?' Mum
demanded.

 'It was Fatty,' I
said, pointing at our
fat lazy cat
sunbathing
in the
middle
of the
lawn.

Fatty opened one eye, hissed at me and then went back to sleep. Even the cat knew Mum wouldn't believe that. Fatty never did *anything* energetic.

LaZY HISS
↘
SSSSZZ!

Mum was too angry to give me the usual lecture about making up stories. Instead she sent me to my room and banned me from the JCHQ until all the flowers had been replaced using my own pocket money. I suppose paying for the damage was only fair, but keeping me out of my writing den was the worst punishment EVER!

The following morning I woke to the sound of Mum calling my name from the garden. I thought she was going to tell me off again or make me start work early, undoing the mess I'd made. But when I came down in my pyjamas and looked out across the garden I saw an amazing sight!

All the borders were filled to
bursting with flowers, even
more flowers than Mum
originally had, and all the *proper*
weeding had been done around them.

'How did this happen?' I said,
scratching my head.

'I thought *you* might be able to tell *me*,'
Mum said smiling, overjoyed to have
her garden looking wonderful again.

She grabbed me and
planted a big wet kiss on my
cheek. 'Thank you, Angel Cake. I don't
know how you did it but you've made
your mother very happy!'

'But . . .' I said helplessly.

'Very happy *indeed*,' she added, and
ran back inside the house before I
could say anything else. Mums
sometimes do this when they don't
want to know something that might
put them back in a bad mood.

She obviously hadn't noticed the tiny
muddy footprints
trailing across
the patio,

goblin ↑
footprints
↓

or that the flower beds in the
neighbours' gardens looked a whole lot
thinner than they had the day before.
Mum did wonder why the potted plant
in the living room had suddenly
shrivelled up and died, but I didn't
think she'd believe me if I told her.

So for once I said nothing and
Mum stayed happy (and I
stayed in her good books).

Because my punishment was over I went straight to the JCHQ to start writing up this story and there was a small note on the desk. In very tiny writing it read:

thankyou FOR THE Weeds

JC

Jake Cake
Productions

JAKE CAKE

AND THE

Tricky
Witch

'**B**ut there's nothing wrong with
the ones I'm wearing!' I
whined, as Mum dragged me down the
busy high street. Although it was far
too late because the ugly new shoes

were already in a box under
Mum's arm.

My only
chance now was
to refuse to
wear them.

'You may
not want
new shoes, Angel Cake, but you
definitely need
them,' Mum said,
pointing an accusing
finger at my
favourite old trainers
as they flipped and
flopped on the
pavement.

Mum's Accusing Finger

Admittedly my old trainers had seen
better days, but they were *so*
comfortable, nearly as comfortable as
my feet, unlike the new ones that
rubbed my ankles and squeaked when
Mum marched me up and down the
shop in them.

Mum stopped abruptly on the
pavement and because I had my head
down in a sulk I nearly ran into her.

We were standing outside
a sweet shop and Mum
was pulling out her
purse, which
could mean
only one
thing.
  Bribery!
  Bribery
only works
one way with
parents. You either take what's on offer
and do as you're told, or refuse what's
    on offer and *still* do as you're told
    because you don't *really* have a
choice. In fact the bribe is only there
to stop kids moaning.

So I took the
money with a
defeated sigh
and went in the
sweet shop.

As I stepped
inside a small
brass bell rang
above my head
and the door
slammed shut

behind me (which by the way is *never*
a good sign), but the smell of sweets
had already filled my nostrils so I kept
on going.

BIG mistake!

As I browsed the shop I got the strange feeling someone was watching me even though there was no one around. Then out of the corner of my eye I saw a tall dark figure rise up from behind the counter, a tall dark figure that came to a very sharp point at the top. Which meant that, unless the shop was owned by a big black traffic cone, I had wandered into a witch's lair! I was about to turn and leg it but my feet were glued to the spot. I did wonder if they were on strike over the horrible new shoes, but then the witch glided out from behind

STUCK!

the counter and started cackling and I realized she must have put a spell on my feet.

Cellar Coven
(a coven is usually
three witches)

I've dealt with witches before. There are loads of them around if you know what to look for (I once found a whole coven living in the cellar, but I'll tell you about that another time). But one sure sign of a witch is the cackling. They *all* cackle.

This one was wearing a pointy hat, pointy boots, black dress, stripy stockings *and* she was cackling, so there was no doubting what she was. What I didn't know was what she was up to.

'What's your name, little boy?' said the witch, drumming her long dirty fingernails on her long hairy chin.

You should never engage a witch in conversation if you can avoid it.

95

They play tricks with words and the next thing you know you're volunteering to climb into their oven or something. But my mouth, like my feet, seemed to have a mind of its own.

'Jake Cake,' I said, while trying my best to say nothing at all.

'Jake *Cake*,' said the witch, pressing her big hooked nose against my head and taking a great noisy sniff of my hair. 'A nice big *Cake* for my oven!' she cackled.

Sniff!

GULP!

I must have gone
pale because the
witch suddenly
threw her head
back and started

cackling even louder. 'Oh, they fall for
it every time!' she shrieked, clapping
her hands together with joy. 'Eating

children
indeed, what
a ridiculous
idea!'

Cackle
Cackle

'You mean
you *don't* eat
children?' I
asked carefully.

97

'YUCK!'

'YUCK!' said the witch, pulling a horrible face (although her face was pretty horrible to begin with). 'Why would anyone want to EAT wretched little children when getting them into trouble is so much more fun.'

'But I'm not in trouble!' I said confidently.

'Wanna bet?' said the witch.

Suddenly a bell rang in the distance followed by a very loud voice.

RING RING

99

'JAKE CAKE, WHAT ON EARTH IS TAKING YOU SO LONG?' Mum yelled, poking her head round the door.

In that moment the witch's spell broke and my feet shot up in the air. I tumbled backwards into the counter with a great CRASH and wound up flat on the floor covered in sweets (which was not as much fun as it sounds).

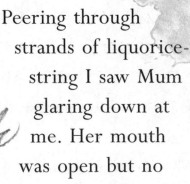

Peering through strands of liquorice-string I saw Mum glaring down at me. Her mouth was open but no words were coming out. At first I thought the witch had cast another spell but the look on Mum's face was a familiar one. It was the look she gets when she's too shocked to speak.

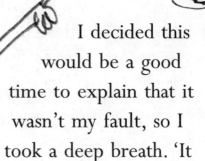

I decided this would be a good time to explain that it wasn't my fault, so I took a deep breath. 'It wasn't me it was the witch and she glued my feet to the floor and she was cackling and said she'd get me into trouble . . .'

But Mum wasn't listening. She had suddenly found her voice again and was making up for lost time.

'Look at all this mess you've made!' she sighed in exasperation. 'Goodness knows what this nice lady thinks of you!'

Nice lady? What nice lady? I couldn't remember seeing a nice lady . . .

Standing next to Mum was the witch, but she was no longer wearing a pointy hat, pointy boots and stripy stockings. Now she was wearing a flowery dress, a knitted shawl and a pair of fluffy slippers. And instead of cackling she was sobbing loudly into a handkerchief.

'Oh, my poor shop!' she sobbed. 'Whatever will I do?'

'Mum, she's not a nice lady!' I yelled. 'She's a WICKED OLD CRONE!'

Mum gasped in horror, grabbed my arm and winched me upright out of the sugary mess.

'You are going to apologize
to Mrs . . .?' Mum gave the
sobbing witch an
embarrassed look.
'Mrs Lovely,' said
the witch. 'My name
is Mrs Lovely.'

I would have burst out laughing if I wasn't in so much trouble.

'You are going to apologize to Mrs Lovely right now, young man,' Mum demanded. '*And* you're going to pay for the damage you've caused. With your own pocket money!' Mum folded her arms and waited.

The witch was peering at me over her soggy handkerchief, her eyes bright and smiling. She was obviously enjoying this. I'm surprised she managed to stop herself from cackling, but that would have given her away.

Mum began tapping her foot impatiently and I knew what I had to do.

'Er . . .' I said, trying to swallow my frustration. 'I'm sorry, Mrs *Lovely*, for messing up your shop.'

The witch considered my apology, gave one last enormous sob into her handkerchief and then nodded graciously. Mum snorted her approval, paid the witch for the ruined sweets and dragged me from the shop.

All the way home Mum gave me the usual lecture about making up stories and how my nose will grow long if I keep it up.

I just nodded in all the right places and said nothing, which is the best thing to do when you're in *that much* trouble.

Mum sent me straight to my room when we got home, although not before binning my favourite old trainers and handing me the ugly new shoes. I even had to hand over the bribe money to start paying Mum back for what she gave the witch.

This was the worst day *ever*, and all because of the tricky witch!

That evening I sat at my computer, looking for clues

of any witch activity in the area, I *had* to prove to Mum that Mrs Lovely was a witch or else I'd be handing over my pocket money for a month!

I'd been searching for ages without any luck when a curious email suddenly popped up on my screen. The sender was anonymous but attached to the email was a scan of a sales receipt:

SALES RECEIPT

ONE CAULDRON
DELIVERED TO: The Sweet Shop
SIGNED FOR BY

Mrs Lovely

I didn't know where the email had come from but someone was obviously trying to help.

Maybe it was another victim of the tricky witch who was too scared to confront her.

The receipt on its own wasn't going to be enough to convince Mum that Mrs Lovely was a witch, but it gave me an idea. If I could *find* the cauldron filled with a magical brew then Mum would *have* to believe me and the witch would be nailed.

I quickly pulled on my ugly new shoes and slid down the drainpipe.

By the time I got to the high street my feet were throbbing from the new shoes, but I managed to hobble down the alleyway to the back of the sweet shop without yelping or being seen. All the lights were out in the shop so I crept up to the rear window and peered inside.

If there was a large cauldron in the back of the shop I couldn't see it. But then I couldn't see much of anything because it was so dark inside. I needed a closer look. Suddenly a strong gust of wind blew through the alleyway and the window I was peering through creaked open.

GULP!

I glanced around to make sure no one was watching and then climbed in through the window.

Landing with a thud, I quickly held my breath. It was so quiet in the back of the shop I could hear my heart pounding like a drum in my chest.

Then, as I crept across the room to search for clues, I heard a terrifying sound.

Squeak!
Squeak!
Squeak!

At first I thought the witch might have a giant mouse guarding the shop, until I realized the sound was coming from my shoes.

SQUEAK! SQUEAK! SQUEAK! they went with every step I took and in the silence of the shop the sound was deafening. But there was nothing I could do. If I took the shoes off, my feet would swell up like balloons and I'd never get them back on again, so instead I tried taking bigger steps and fewer of them.

SQUEAK! SQUEAK! SQUEAK!

Then I heard another sound, but this time it wasn't coming from my shoes, it came from a small dark shadow in the doorway across the room. A small dark shadow with bright-green eyes . . .

MeeeeaaaW!

The black cat leapt through the air, pounced on my shoes and started attacking them with its claws!

I obviously wasn't alone in thinking they sounded like mice. But my noisy shoes were nothing compared to the racket the cat was making. It screeched and howled and leapt up and down on my feet, swiping with its paws and chewing on my laces!

Suddenly a light came on in the room, the cat scarpered and the witch was hovering in the doorway on her broomstick. She wore a long black dressing gown, black pointy slippers and a floppy pointy hat that was obviously just for sleeping in.

'Jake *Cake.*' She smiled, but it wasn't a nice smile, it was a sly witchy smile.

With the light on I could see the room properly. There *was* a large cauldron in the middle of the room and it was filled with a mysterious, hubbling-bubbling witch's brew.

'Aha!' I said.

'Aha?' said the witch, whooshing over to the cauldron on her broom.

'Yes, aha!' I said triumphantly. 'Now I've got proof that you're cooking up spells, you're so completely BUSTED!'

The witch dipped her finger into the cauldron, pulled out a big glob of brown goo and popped it in her mouth.

'You have proof that I've cooked up a big pot of *toffee*,' she corrected.

'Toffee?'

'Yes,' said the witch. 'Toffee in a sweet shop, how peculiar!'

'It's probably *magic* toffee!' I said. 'You're cooking up *magic* toffee that turns kids into frogs or gives them warts or something!'

'No. It's just toffee,' said the witch, hopping off her broomstick and lifting up a big crate of apples. 'Toffee for toffee apples.'

'Then they must be *poisoned* apples!' I said. 'Everyone knows about witches and poisoned apples. It's not even very original.'

'No, they're just regular apples.'

The witch picked up one of the apples and took a big bite to prove her point. 'Just regular toffee and regular apples.'

CHOMP CHOMP

'Regular toffee apples?' I asked suspiciously.

'Yes,' said the witch with a mischievous smile. 'So if you're looking for proof of spells to get you out of trouble you're out of luck.'

'But you stuck my feet to the floor with a spell!' I said.

'No, I didn't,' she said. 'The floor is just very sticky around the counter.'

I gave the witch a look that said I didn't believe a word she was saying.

'I just enjoy getting children into trouble,' said the witch. 'But I don't need to cast spells to do that. You're in trouble right now and I didn't use any magic at all.'

'Aha!' I said, and this time I was certain that I had the upper hand. 'Mum doesn't even know I'm here, so I'm not even *in* trouble, so there!'

'Wrong again,' said the witch. 'I'm afraid your mum is already on her way.'

122

GULP!

The witch began rummaging
inside her long black robe.

Did she have a voodoo doll with a pin
in its bottom to wake Mum and bring
her here? Or maybe an enchanted crow
that had flown on dark wings with a
message of my whereabouts? One thing
was certain: if Mum *was* on her way it
was because of something foul and
wicked and definitely witchy!

The witch grinned
as she produced the
magical device of
my downfall. And
do you know what it
was? A mobile phone!

123

It wasn't even a black mobile phone with bats on it, it was bright pink with flowers on it and glitter round the edge!

'Well, you couldn't have got the number without using some kind of spell!' I said, still desperately looking for proof of witchcraft.

The witch rummaged inside her robe again and pulled out a laptop!

'No, I just used the online phone directory,' she said with an even bigger grin.

'As an experienced hacker I do find technology *so* much more reliable than herbs and potions, and practically impossible to prove!'

'So it was *you* who sent the email to lure me here?' I said, feeling well and truly tricked.

The witch nodded.

In the distance a small bell

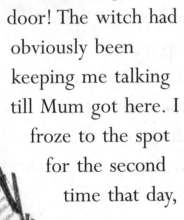

RING
RING

rang above the shop door! The witch had obviously been keeping me talking till Mum got here. I froze to the spot for the second time that day,

but it wasn't a spell *or* a sticky carpet.
This time it was sheer dread.

As Mum's footsteps made their way
through the shop I looked down at
my feet, willing them to leg it. It was

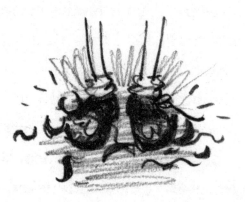

then that I noticed the witch's cat had
completely wrecked my new shoes.
They lay in scraps around my feet
as if they'd been through a
paper shredder!

Although I was already in trouble,
I suddenly realized I was about to get
proof of some witchcraft. Mum was on
her way and the witch still looked like
a witch!

Our eyes locked across the room.
I had her! She would have to do some
magic to get out of this one!

The witch raised an eyebrow as
Mum's footsteps grew closer. Then, in
a flurry of activity, she whipped off her
hat and dressing gown and kicked off
her witchy slippers.

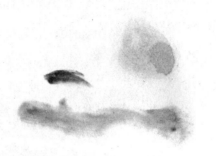

Bundle of
Witchy
Clothes
↙

Underneath the witch clothes she
was dressed as an old lady again.

The witch threw the ball of black
cloth into the corner of the room and
produced another soggy handkerchief.

'Do come and visit me again, Jake
Cake. It's been *so much* fun!' she
cackled, and then began sobbing at the

top of her voice.
Mum also used the
top of her voice
when she found
me, and because
we've been here
many times
before I don't
need to tell you
exactly what she
said, except to say that I was
in SO MUCH TROUBLE!

The next day I sat in
my room, where I
would be spending a
very long time because
I was completely
grounded. The only company I had
was our cat Fatty (who doesn't really
like me). He waddled into my room,
swiped at the tatty shoelace of my

tatty old trainers and collapsed into an exhausted heap at my very comfortable feet.

OK, the witch *had* totally outsmarted me (I told you they were tricky), but because her cat wrecked my squeaky new shoes Mum was forced to fish out the old ones from the bin.

So I think maybe me and the witch
are even.

Until the next time . . .

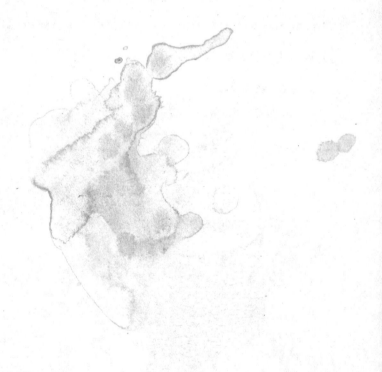

JC
Jake Cake
Productions

UNBELIEVABLE ADVENTURE REPORT

OFFICIAL JC DOCUMENT

NAME: Robot Dinner Lady (Mrs Brown)

AGE: Just a couple of weeks since Mrs WINTER finished her!

WEIGHT: about the same as a CAR! (very heavy)

How To Spot One They're made of metal and sometimes their heads fall off. oops!

Comments: I suppose there are lots of different kinds of Robots. My one is ok now she can cook CHIPS - but I didn't like her much when she only cooked Cabbage! And it was the slimy CABBAGE that made her go MENTAL! So Cabbage and ROBOTS don't mix.

JC
Jake Cake
Productions

UNBELIEVABLE ADVENTURE REPORT

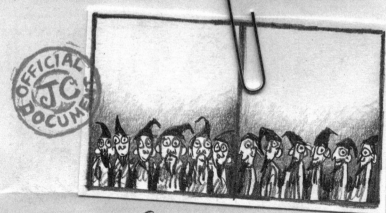

OFFICIAL JC DOCUMENT

NAME: Goblins (don't know the names of them all)

AGE: they're probably all different ages.

WEIGHT: about the same as a bag of crisps.

How To Spot One. They're small and hard to spot, so look for a **BIG MESS** and you'll probably find a goblin or six.

Comments: Don't make a deal with them or you might end up with an empty garden and wee in a plant pot (I think he thought it was a plant potty!)

JC Jake Cake Productions

UNBELIEVABLE ADVENTURE REPORT

NAME: Tricky Witch (Mrs Lovely - yeah right!)

AGE: Witches can be hundreds of years old!
(which is why they're so ugly!)

WEIGHT: Weightless when on a broomstick!

How To Spot One. Pointy hat - warts - hooky nose
(and they ALWAYS cackle)

Comments: The tricky witch still has her
sweetshop - so I'd better keep an
eye out for witchy activities. I
don't think I've seen the last of her.
(but I'll be prepared next time!)

JC
Jake Cake
Productions

'cackle'
'cackle'

Read all the unbelievable adventures of

JAKE CAKE

that's me ↑

I did all the writing and all the drawing